SCOOBY-DOO!
VALENTINE'S DAY DOGNAPPING

By Gail Herman
Illustrated by Duendes del Sur

D0172049

SCHOLASTIC INC.
New York   Toronto   London   Auckland   Sydney
Mexico City   New Delhi   Hong Kong   Buenos Aires

ISBN 0-439-34113-2

12 11   8 9/0

Designed by Maria Stasavage
Printed in the U.S.A.
First Scholastic printing, January 2002

The gang was at a new pizza place.
Scooby-Doo nosed a menu across the table.
"Like, hurry up and order!" Shaggy told
Velma, Daphne, and Fred. "This place is about
to close!"

THREE SISTERS
GRAND
OPENING

*Happy
Valentine's
Day*

Soon, everyone got their pizzas.

"Hey!" said Shaggy, surprised.

"What's with the heart shapes?"

"It's Valentine's Day," Velma told him.

"Rovey-Dovey!" Scooby said. "Rew!"

"Scoob doesn't like mushy stuff."
Shaggy laughed. "Unless it's food,
right old buddy?" He waited for
an answer. "Old buddy?"

Scooby was staring at a dainty dog.
"I think Scooby is in love!" said Daphne.
Fred walked over to the dog, and read
her name tag.
"Hello, Prissy," he said.
"Meet our friend Scooby-Doo!"

The dog turned and scooted under the counter.

Then she poked her nose over. "Like, she's playing with you, Scoob," said Shaggy.

All at once, somebody scooped her up. Prissy howled as she was whisked away.

"Like, that dog's in trouble!" Shaggy declared.
Scooby jumped up.
Then he jumped back.
He gobbled the last pizza crumbs.
Then he took off again.

Scooby chased Prissy.

Shaggy chased Scooby.

And the rest of the gang chased Shaggy.

Down the block, Scooby skidded to a stop.

Crash! Shaggy ran into Scooby, and Velma, Fred, and Daphne ran into Shaggy.
When they all stood up, they saw a woman wearing dark robes.
She was disappearing inside a spooky old house — with Prissy!

"That woman looks like a witch!" Shaggy told Scooby.

"And your main squeeze has been doggynapped!"

"Roh no!" cried Scooby.

Velma shook her head. "Wait a
minute, you guys. Why would a
witch want a dog? Shouldn't she
have a cat?"

"Meow!" A black cat darted
into the house.

13

Scooby howled.

"Poor Scooby," said Daphne.

"We've got to help him — and Prissy,"
Velma agreed.

"Come on, everyone," said Fred.

"The door is still open."

Inside, everyone tiptoed through the dark rooms.
Cobwebs hung from the ceiling.
Everything was old and dusty.

"This way," said Shaggy.

"Ooph!" He tripped over a broom.

"Zoinks!" he cried loudly. "A witch's broom!"

"Drusilla?" called a voice. "Ludwinka? Is that you?"

Everyone froze.

But then two voices called back,
"Yes, it's us."
"More witches!" Shaggy whispered.

Quietly, the gang peeked into the kitchen. The witches were stirring something in a huge cauldron.

"It's almost ready," cackled the first witch, Prunella.

"Just one more ingredient . . ."

"Uh-oh," groaned Shaggy. "You don't think she means —"

"Rissy!" Scooby finished.

"We've got to find that dog!" said Daphne.

"Right," Fred said. "Let's split up."

Velma led Fred and Daphne upstairs.

Scooby and Shaggy slipped into the kitchen and down the basement stairs.

In the dim light, they saw shelves lined with jars.

"Potion ingredients," Shaggy whispered. He picked up one jar.

"Worms!" He picked up another one.

"Eyeballs!"

"Like, ugh!" Shaggy said, dropping the jars
and racing up the stairs.

"Rait for me!" shouted Scooby.

Thud, thud, thud!

They weren't quiet now!

"What's going on?" said Prunella.

Scooby and Shaggy swept past her.

"This way!" said Shaggy.

Crash! They ran into Ludwinka.

"No, the other way!" Shaggy shouted.

Crash! They ran into Drusilla.

"Like, hide Scoob!" Shaggy cried. "Here!"
They dove into the cauldron.

Seconds later, they came up for air.
"Whew," said Shaggy. Velma, Fred, and
Daphne were racing to the rescue.
But the witches were right behind!
Shaggy gulped. He gulped again.
"Like, this is some tasty brew!"

Velma peered into the cauldron. "This isn't brew!" she exclaimed. "It's pizza sauce!"

She looked closely at the witches. "I've seen your picture on the menu from the pizza place. You're the three sisters, from the Three Sisters Restaurant!"

"But they *are* witches!" said Shaggy.
"Scoob and I saw jars of eyeballs
and worms."

Velma laughed. "That must be olives
and pasta — for the restaurant!"

Prunella held up the menu for Shaggy.
"But what about the brooms? The black
cat?" he said.
"We just moved here," Prunella said. "And
we're trying to clean the place up."

"That's why you have so many brooms!"
Daphne said.
Then Prunella rubbed the cat's back.
The black came off.
"It's dust!" exclaimed Fred.

Scooby howled. "Rissy!"

"That's right," said Shaggy.

"You stole Scooby's love-doggy!"

"Prissy is our dog," explained Drusilla.
"But she didn't want to come here.
She doesn't like anything dirty."

Just then Prissy padded in. She smiled at
Scooby.

Then Prissy saw the sauce on Scooby. She stopped smiling. "Humph!" She turned away.

Scooby shrugged and smiled.
He'd already found a new love.
The pizza sauce!
"Scooby-Dooby-Doo!" he said.